The Emperor's New Clothes

Story by:
Hans Christian Andersen

Adapted by:
Margaret Ann Hughes

Illustrated by:

Russell Hicks	Lorann Downer
Theresa Mazurek	Rivka
Douglas McCarthy	Fay Whitemountain
Allyn Conley-Gorniak	Suzanne Lewis
Julie Ann Armstrong	

This Book Belongs To:

Use this symbol to match book and cassette.

nce upon a time, in a far off land, there lived an emperor.

Now the emperor loved his people…almost as much as he loved new clothes. He loved clothes more than anything in the world. When he wasn't at court, or with his council, the emperor was in his closet looking at his clothes.

One day two peddlers, named Hoodwink and Possum, came to the village. There they heard of the emperor who loved new clothes. Eager to make money, but not caring how, Hoodwink had an idea.

They disguised themselves as tailors. Then they took two empty suitcases and went to the palace, where they were brought before the emperor and his court.

Hoodwink and Possum told the emperor about a special suit that only they could make.

The tailors said that with the magic thread they had in their suitcases they could weave a special cloth—a cloth they could make into a magic suit. And what made the suit so magic? Why, they said, only people who were WISE could see the suit…and FOOLS could not!

The emperor liked the idea of a magic suit, especially since it would be the only one of its kind.

So, he ordered the tailors to begin the suit right away.

The emperor agreed to give the tailors whatever they needed to make the suit.

Hoodwink and Possum asked for a room, with a loom and gold, to do their work. The tribune saw to it that the tailors were given all they asked for. Then he left them alone with the gold and the looms.

So the Two Tailors of Tuddle began their work. They made broad gestures with their hands and worked the looms back and forth, pretending to make cloth.

Hoodwink and Possum worked day and night on the magic suit. The emperor would not let anyone disturb them, so no one ever entered their room. As servants passed in the halls, they could hear the looms busy at work as the tailors hummed along. Everyone tried to imagine what the magic suit was like.

Now the emperor had promised that he wouldn't peek until the suit was finished. But finally, he just couldn't wait any longer. He called to his tribune and asked him to check on the progress of the suit.

The tribune did as he was asked and went to the room where the suit was being made. There he saw Hoodwink and Possum waving their arms and moving a needle in and out of the air.

The tailors stopped working and showed the tribune the unfinished magic suit.

The tribune looked, then rubbed his eyes, and then he looked again. But he just didn't see a suit of any kind…unfinished or otherwise! Could he be a fool? Why, he could lose his job! Quickly he convinced himself that he could really see…oh, dear…the magic suit of clothes.

The tribune gave the tailors two more bags of gold to make a matching jacket. Then he left them busily working on the suit.

So, the tribune returned to the emperor with a glowing report on the new suit. Of course, he couldn't really say he hadn't seen the suit. The tribune was too ashamed to admit that he must be a fool.

Well, with such a fine report, the emperor was even more pleased.

Plans were made for a grand and glorious parade. The villagers put up banners and cleaned the streets to make ready for the emperor the next day. Everyone had heard about the magic suit that only the WISE could see.

The emperor hardly slept at all that night because he was so excited. Finally it was morning. As the villagers lined the streets…the emperor prepared for the parade. He took a bath, trimmed his beard, and sprayed himself with lilac water.

The emperor put on his bathrobe. Then, followed by his tribune and all the other members of his court, he went to the tailor's to dress in his new suit of clothes.

They opened the door and entered…and there stood Hoodwink and Possum, holding up the wonderful magic suit.

Well, I need not tell you that there really was no suit of clothes for them to see.

Then all eyes turned to the emperor. What was he to do? They all seemed to see the suit…but he saw nothing! Was the emperor a fool? They all waited for him to speak.

The emperor was pleased!

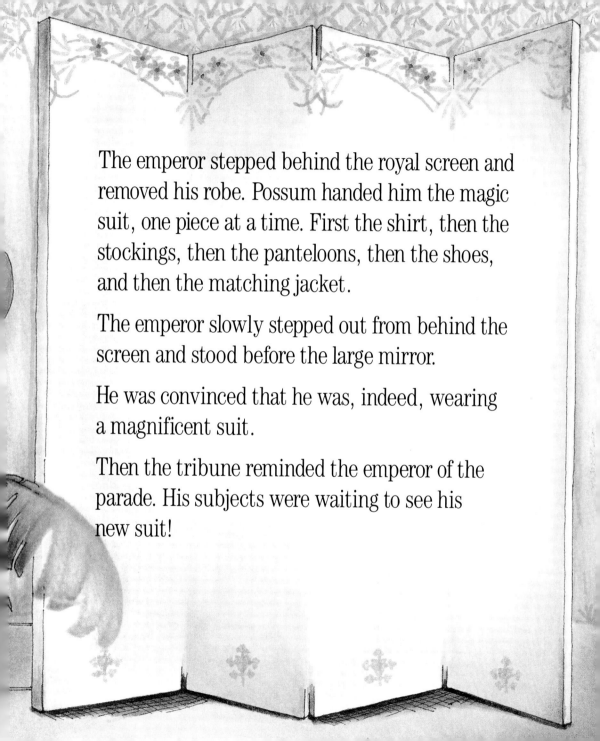

The emperor stepped behind the royal screen and removed his robe. Possum handed him the magic suit, one piece at a time. First the shirt, then the stockings, then the panteloons, then the shoes, and then the matching jacket.

The emperor slowly stepped out from behind the screen and stood before the large mirror.

He was convinced that he was, indeed, wearing a magnificent suit.

Then the tribune reminded the emperor of the parade. His subjects were waiting to see his new suit!

Followed by his tribune and his court, the emperor marched out of the room, down the long hall, through the palace doors, and out into the street. The villagers cheered when they saw him.

Of course, no one wanted to appear foolish!

The emperor marched proudly, nodding to his subjects as he made his way past the cheering crowd.

But as he turned a corner, the cheers were suddenly hushed by one little boy, a poor little boy, named Jason, who shouted…

…the emperor wasn't wearing any clothes!
Oh, my! They all held their breath as the emperor
stopped and stared at the little boy.

The villagers cried out that the boy was a fool!

The emperor realized that Jason was right.
He wasn't wearing any clothes.

The emperor quickly asked to borrow the tribune's cape, then wrapped it all around himself.

The emperor continued to march in his parade, but he quickened his pace, marching just a little faster than he had before.

After the parade, Jason was brought to the palace. He had no idea what the emperor would say to him.

Jason was asked to hold out his hand. Then the emperor dropped a handful of coins into it.

And so, Jason was rewarded for pointing out how foolish the emperor had been. As for Hoodwink and Possum, they had slipped away some time during the parade. And you can be sure, they never returned to that village again.

But in a way, what they had said was true. The magic suit really did show who was wise and who was foolish. And because the emperor admitted how foolish he had been, he was very wise after all.

 nd they all lived happily ever after.